Frances P. Cobbe, Benjamin Bryan

Vivisection in America

I. How it is taught II. How it is practised

Frances P. Cobbe, Benjamin Bryan

Vivisection in America
I. How it is taught II. How it is practised

ISBN/EAN: 9783337255909

Printed in Europe, USA, Canada, Australia, Japan

Cover: Foto ©Andreas Hilbeck / pixelio.de

More available books at **www.hansebooks.com**

FOR THE PROTECTION OF ANIMALS FROM VIVISECTION.

VIVISECTION IN AMERICA.

I.—HOW IT IS TAUGHT.
II.—HOW IT IS PRACTISED.

BY

FRANCES POWER COBBE

AND

BENJAMIN BRYAN.

LONDON:
SWAN, SONNENSCHEIN AND CO., PATERNOSTER SQUARE,
ALSO OFFICES OF THE VICTORIA STREET SOCIETY,
20, VICTORIA STREET, LONDON;
AND THROUGH ALL BOOKSELLERS.
FOURTH EDITION.
1890.

PREFACE TO THE FOURTH EDITION.

THAT the subject of Vivisection is one of importance
and interest, especially at the present day, in view
of its surprising increase during the past ten years, is
attested by the fact that the letters to the undersigned
herein reproduced are written by representative men and
women of universal fame, and in many cases of widely
diverse views.

When persons of the exalted character of Rev. Dr.
Bartol; Dr. Berdoe, of England; Dr. Blackwood; United
States Senator Blair; Rev. Dr. Phillips Brooks; United
States Senator Chandler; Miss Frances Power Cobbe;
Miss Fanny Davenport; United States Senator Dawes;
Rev. Dr. Morgan Dix; United States Senator Dolph; Mr.
William Lloyd Garrison; Col. Robert G. Ingersoll; Mme.
Ouida; Mme. Adelina Patti; Signor Salvini; Mr. Denman
Thompson; Baron von Weber, of Germany; and a large
number of others, whose letters it would be impossible to
publish for want of space, — people illustrious in their
various walks of life, and who are far from being " senti-
mentalists," — are willing to place themselves on record as
opposed to this frightful practice (and nearly all even un-
qualifiedly advocating its absolute prohibition), we may
well pause to question the utility and propriety of Vivisection.

The undersigned, who has made a careful study of the
subject during more than fifteen years, and who has
derived the knowledge he possesses of the matter from the
works of the vivisectors themselves, and not from the

writings of their opponents, — so that, if he be partisan, his partisanship must be on the side of the former, in whose interest he originally worked until he ascertained the truth — has no hesitation in positively stating that it has not only not been productive of good, but that it has proved a most prolific source of error; and none have been more ready to admit this than many of the great vivisectors. It is said that Majendie, the "Prince of Torturers," when ill, persistently refused to be attended by any physician who had drawn his conclusions from a source so certain to lead to error as Vivisection.

It has been abundantly proven by the experience of the Victoria Street Society of England that no possible restrictive law, so-called, will be of the slightest benefit.

About fourteen years ago, after long and conscientious labor, a number of prominent philanthropists, chief among whom was, I believe, my friend Miss Frances Power Cobbe, succeeded in having a restrictive law enacted by Parliament, which at the time promised much. The results were embodied in a pamphlet published about two years ago, called "Twelve Years' Trial of the Vivisection Act." It was therein shown not only that the practice of Vivisection had not been diminished, but that it had *flourished more than ever before*, under the so-called restrictive act, which was valuable to the vivisectors, principally by being an absolute shield and bulwark to all who complied with the provisions which "restricted," the principal clause of which required them to take out licenses before vivisecting.

"It was not till nearly four years' experience of parliamentary action on the subject, and of very arduous and painful study, that the program of restriction was finally abandoned by the originators of the movement." No restrictive act which human ingenuity may devise can afford sufficient protection to animals delivered over to a vivisection. Some opponents of vivisection fondly imagine that they can devise such provisions; but it can be unhesitatingly asserted that no one who understands the purposes and methods of vivisectional research can believe that such provisions are possible. They fall back on the old fallacy of anæsthetics; of this it is sufficient to quote the famous words of Dr. Hoggan: "Anæsthetics" (by the delusions which humane people indulge about them) "have proved the greatest curse to vivisectible animals."

There can be absolutely no line drawn by the Legislature between the use of vivisection and its worst abuses; and "whenever the abuses of a practice are very great, and they cannot be separated from the use, then the use itself must be forbidden," according to a well-recognized principle of legislation.

Perhaps the greatest of all incentives to vivisection is the honor (?) and distinction obtained among the vivisectors by the published accounts of their exploits. So long as it is permitted under a restrictive law, so long such publications (with due care in alleging the use of anæsthetics, and compliance with other provisions of law) may safely go on. But if it be forbidden unconditionally, then, and then only, this great incentive to the practice will cease to exist.

Rather than cause the enactment of a restrictive law in the United States, the best-informed opponents of Vivisection would defer all legislation on the subject until, through continued agitation, by the introduction of bills for its total suppression in the State legislatures and in Congress, and in every other possible way, the time shall arrive when the approach of civilization will make it possible for such bills to become laws; which laws, in a civilized age, there would never be occasion to invoke.

There is another phase of the subject as yet but little thought of. *There is no argument in favor of Vivisection which does not apply more completely, more forcibly, to men than to animals.* If the inferior is justly sacrificed to the higher, the legality of the surrender to scientific torture of idiots, criminals, those incurably diseased, and, indeed, all ignorant and brutalized men, including vivisectors, is beyond question. The lives of these are valueless to society, when they are not, as they usually are, noxious to it. At present vivisectors are timid and hypocritical. They sigh that the "rat or two" that they ask in their love for humanity is grudgingly bestowed; but they do not mention so freely the hundreds of experiments in which they keep animals skinned, with nerves laid bare, irritated with electricity and in every possible way, cut open their living bodies, roast, crucify, boil, subject them to experiments causing the most excruciating agony in the most sensitive nerves — and the greater the suffering the greater the "joyful excitement" with which they inflict it. They already say among themselves that no true results can be reached *without human subjects.*

"French and Italian physiologists outrival each other in their relations of their wanton and exultant ingenuity in producing unnatural agony and watching its helpless struggles," says "Ouida," to whom the writer is indebted for many of the facts herein appearing. "That these men do not immediately give themselves the greater luxury of human victims is due only to their timidity before public opinion. I fail to see any logical refusal that can be made them when they shall demand it." When Majendie, ope-rating for cataract, plunged his needle to the bottom of his patient's eye, that he might observe the effect of mechanical irritation of the retina upon unexpectant nerves, he showed how greatly the zeal of the vivisector may impair the conscientiousness of the medical adviser, and, above all, the sympathy of man for man. No wonder that vivisectors refuse to be attended, when ill, by vivisectors !

Liberty in Vivisection, physiologists themselves, in Ger-many, France, and Italy, say, has produced abuses. In

America, says Dr. Leffingwell, it has led to the repetition, *for demonstration*, of Majendie's extreme barbarities, — barbarities which have been condemned by every leading physiologist of England, in which country a careful study of mortality statistics shows that in no case has Vivisection lessened the fatality of a single disease beyond what it was thirty-five years ago.

In ten years Prof. Schiff vivisected fourteen thousand (14,000) dogs; it is estimated that of other animals he vivisected seventy thousand (70,000); and ten years ago he was regularly calling for ten dogs a week. At that time, in Lyons, dogs were becoming scarce, and it was proposed to breed them for the purpose of Vivisection.

Mr. Murdock, a most able veterinary surgeon, in a work published by him, gives an account of a visit to a French laboratory as follows: "Here lay six or seven living horses, fixed by every mechanical device by the head and feet to pillars, while the students were engaged in performing different operations. The sight was truly horrible! The operations had begun early in the forenoon, it now being three o'clock. . . . The poor wretches had ceased being able to make any violent struggles; but the deep heaving of the panting chest, and the horrid look of the eyes, when such were yet left in the head, the head itself being lashed to a pillar, was harrowing beyond endurance.

"The students had begun their day's work in the least vital parts of the animals. The trunks were there, but they had lost their tails, hoofs, ears, etc.; and the operators were now engaged in the more important operations, such as tying the arteries, trepanning the cranium, cutting down upon the sensitive parts, — as we were informed, on expressing our horror, that they might see the retraction of the muscles by pinching and irritating the various nerves.

"One animal had a side of the head, including the eye

and ear, completely dissected; and other students were laying open and cauterizing the hock of the same animal."

Mr. Rogers adds to this : —

"The number of horses operated on is six, twice a week ; sixty-four operations are performed on *each horse*, and four or five generally die before half the operations are completed ; and, as it takes two days to go through the list, the remaining one or two poor animals are left alive, half-mangled, until the next morning, only to be subjected to additional tortures.

"Among the operations which I remember, were firing in every part where it could or could not be required ; operation for removing the lateral cartilages, which involves tearing off the quarters of the hoof with pincers ; operation for stone, in which a stone is put into the bladder and afterwards removed ; operation for hernia, nicking, removal of the ears, eyes, etc.

"The effect of all this on the minds of the students may be inferred from the *sang froid* of a student who was firing a horse's nose, as he said, for pastime.

"A little bay mare, worn out in the service of man, one of eight, on a certain operation day, having unfortunately retained life throughout the fiendish ordeal, and looking like nothing ever made by the hand of God,—with loins ripped open, skin torn and ploughed by red-hot irons, riddled by setons, tendons severed, hoofless, sightless, and defenceless, was exultingly reared [Baron von Weber says, 'amid laughter'] on her bleeding feet just when gasping for breath and dying, to show what *dexterity* had done in completing its work before death took place."

Is it surprising that the late Henry Bergh considered that this unfitted "the physician for the intimate and tender relations of friend and adviser," and made him " hence more to be dreaded than disease itself"?

Below follows a letter similar to those sent to a number of prominent persons : —

OFFICE OF PHILIP G. PEABODY.

ATTORNEY AND COUNSELOR-AT-LAW,

BOSTON, MASS., March 20, 1890.

To

MY DEAR SIR :

Permit me, at the suggestion of my friend, Mr. George T. Angell, President of the Mass. Society for the Prevention of Cruelty to Animals, to respectfully direct your attention to the subject matter of this pamphlet, which I take the liberty of forwarding you, and to beg the favor of its thoughtful perusal at your hands.

If the most cruel and unjustifiable exercise imaginable of the power possessed by the strong to oppress the weak can move your heart to pity, the case as herein presented surely cannot fail to do so, for it faithfully portrays those cruelties, terrible even beyond mortal conception, to which defenceless animals are daily subjected in the United States, at the hands of merciless vivisectors — in other words, animals are dissected alive, usually without the use of anæsthetics, for the supposed (but illusory) gain to science.

Being about to issue at my own expense (and, I may add, wholly without the possibility of pecuniary emolument resulting therefrom, or even reimbursement), a very large edition of the pamphlet, " Vivisection in America," I beg of you most earnestly to forward to me your written endorsement and approval of its purpose, that I may, with your kind permission, print the same in connection with words of commendation from other representative persons, in a preface to the new edition.

By so doing you will materially advance the cause of Humanity, and incur the profound and lasting gratitude of all lovers of Justice.

Permit me, my dear Sir, to subscribe myself,

Yours truly,

PHILIP G. PEABODY,

No. 18 Richfield Street.

In reply to this, the letters printed below (with the exception of the first) have been received in the order in which they are printed : —

From the late Henry Bergh, founder, and for nearly twenty-two years president, of the American Society for the Prevention of Cruelty to Animals : —

THE AMERICAN SOCIETY FOR THE PREVENTION OF CRUELTY TO ANIMALS,
HEADQUARTERS OF THE SOCIETY,
FOURTH AVE., COR. 22D ST., NEW YORK, *Sept. 2, 1880.*

PHILIP G. PEABODY, Esq. :

Dear Sir, — Your favor is received, in relation to vivisection. *After long and patient investigation* of the subject, and in view of the action of the people of several European states — recommending the *total* abolition of the hideous practice — I last winter asked to be heard by the Legislature of New York upon the propriety of its entire prohibition. A memorial prepared by me was presented simultaneously and read in both houses, and referred to a joint committee. That committee appointed the assembly chamber for a hearing ; and, having previously made myself master of my subject, I laid bare the awful features of it.

The *Herald* and other papers next day testified to the thoroughness of the manner in which it was treated ; but the bill afterwards presented was rejected by Senate and Assembly.

This I expected, as I never contemplated doing more than to exhibit to the people the barbarities which are going on in their midst in the insulted name of Science ! reserving for a future occasion more practical and positive results.

I have now prepared a printed circular to all our agents throughout the State, instructing them to obtain as many signatures as possible, which at the proper time I shall present to the Legislature, in support of a second application for a law suppressing the dreadful tortures. I may fail again, but I propose to fight this question out on this line, if it takes all the rest of my life !

I believe that these scientific cruelties surpass all other wrongs inflicted on the lower animals — collectively.

To perpetuate them it is first necessary to render the heart as tough and as insensible as India-rubber, which process, I hold, unfits the physician for the intimate and tender relations of friend and adviser, and hence more to be dreaded than disease itself.

The article to which you allude, in the Scribner monthly, I saw, and has been the cause of much public writing in rejoinder, both on my part, and that of scientific men.

It will give me pleasure to confer with you at any time ; and with that view I will state that I am usually at these headquarters daily, except about the middle of the day, when, between 12 and 2, I am in the habit of going out on business. I will be glad to see you here, or, if you prefer, will call on you.

With great respect,
HENRY BERGH.

From Mme. Adelina Patti : —

PARKER HOUSE, SCHOOL ST., CORNER OF TREMONT,
BOSTON, <i>21 Mars, 1890.</i></div>

MONSIEUR :

Etant très occupés en ce moment, Madame Patti vous prie de l'excuser si elle ne répond par directement à votre intéressante lettre, et me charge de vous de vous dire qu'elle adhère complètement aux sentiments de réprobation que vous exprimez sur la vivisection et en général sur toute cruauté envers les animaux.

Veuillez agréer, Monsieur, l'expression de sa considération très distinguée.

Votre humble serviteur,
A. MORINI, <i>Secrétaire.</i></div>

[TRANSLATION.]

PARKER HOUSE, SCHOOL ST., CORNER OF TREMONT,
BOSTON, <i>21st March, 1890.</i></div>

SIR :

Being very occupied at this moment, Madame Patti prays you to excuse her if she does not respond directly to your interesting letter, and charges me to say to you that she adheres completely to the sentiments of reprobation that you express on vivisection and in general on all cruelty toward animals.

Be good enough to receive, Sir, the expression of her very distinguished consideration.

Your humble servant,

A. MORINI, *Secretary.*

From Dr. Blackwood, the eminent physician of Philadelphia :—

246 NORTH 20TH STREET,
PHILADELPHIA, *March 20, 1890.*

MY DEAR SIR :

Your letter has just been handed to me by my friend Mrs. White, and I answer it at once by saying that I endorse all that you advance concerning the brutalizing effect of vivisection on those who prosecute it and the witnesses alike. Absolutely useless as it has been abundantly proved to be to all thinking and reasoning minds, it needs but the careful investigation of the medical profession at large to bring its members to the conclusion reached by the few who have given this important matter the consideration it deserves. I hope the widespread dissemination of the pamphlet *Vivisection in America*, which you propose so generously sending out, will be the means of starting public investigation, and if it does this, the time will soon come when vivisectors will be relegated to the category of professional criminals, and criminals who deserve the heavy hand of the law to be laid on — and laid on the more because they should, from the pretensions they make, be the protectors, instead of the atrocious torturers, of animals who have not the power to protect themselves. With much regard, I am,

Very sincerely yours,

WM. R. D. BLACKWOOD.

PHILIP G. PEABODY, Esq., Boston, Mass.

From Mr. William Lloyd Garrison : —

W. L. GARRISON & CO.,
DEALERS IN
COMMERCIAL PAPER AND WESTERN MORTGAGES,
132 FEDERAL STREET,
BOSTON, *March 21, 1890.*

PHILIP G. PEABODY, Esq.,
Boston, Mass.

MY DEAR SIR :

I have read with painful interest the pamphlet on vivisection which you sent me, and thank you for it.

It seems incredible that men who are working in the interests of mankind can be so cruel and insensible to the sufferings of dumb animals. The contention of the physicians that vivisection has yielded immensely to the knowledge of the human system is by no means made clear, and their claims for alleviating suffering in consequence are to be taken with many grains of allowance. If the verdict of the doctors themselves were unanimous, their case would be a strong one, but with such eminent testimony as that of Dr. Tait against the practice, the question is an open one.

But even though it were demonstrated that medical science had advanced and human suffering been alleviated by the torture of animals, the moral feeling of mankind has yet to be changed before it can accept relief at such a cost. Every feeling of humanity revolts at the experiments as described by the medical men who practise vivisection, and one rises from a perusal of their records with a doubt as to which is the human and which is the brute animal.

I hope your pamphlet will have a wide circulation and an equally wide perusal.

Very sincerely yours,
WM. LLOYD GARRISON.

From Rev. Phillips Brooks : —

233 CLARENDON ST., BOSTON, *March 22, 1890.*

MY DEAR SIR :

I am heartily in sympathy with every wise effort to limit the license of vivisection and to lessen the suffering which it involves, and I sincerely hope that your pamphlet may make valuable contribution to these ends.

Yours very truly,

PHILLIPS BROOKS.

PHILIP G. PEABODY, Esq.

From Senator Dawes, of Massachusetts.

UNITED STATES SENATE,
WASHINGTON, D. C., *24th March, 1890.*

DEAR SIR :

I have yours of the 20th inst., and also your pamphlet, which I have read with great interest and instruction. I agree with you essentially in the suggestions made.

Yours truly,

H. L. DAWES.

PHILIP G. PEABODY, Esq.

From Signor Tommaso Salvini :—

BOSTON, *March 25th, 1890.*

PHILIP G. PEABODY, Esq. :

Dear Sir, — The spirit that animates the Society for the Prevention of Cruelty to Animals, of which you are a worthy representative, can only be the inspiration of a kindly heart, and like you I deplore the fact that these creatures, deprived of speech, but not of feeling and affection, are often sacrificed for anatomical experiments and for other researches of modern science. Those who employ such heartless measures say that these are necessary for the good of humanity, but I repeat instead that they are expedients of a barbarous ambition. Pure science should be of general benefit, hurtful to no one, and in my opinion man should be prevented from the employment of such examples, humiliating to the entire human race.

Very truly yours,

TOMMASO SALVINI.

From Senator Blair, of New Hampshire : —

UNITED STATES SENATE,
WASHINGTON, D. C., *March 29, 1890.*

PHILIP G. PEABODY, Esq.,
Attorney and Counsellor-at-Law, Boston, Mass. :

Dear Sir, — I am in receipt of your pamphlet treating of the barbarities and fiendish cruelties which our Christian civilization practises or permits upon dumb animals. It seems to me that it would be far better that the law should select certain men to die under the knife in the interests of science for humanity in general, just as others are designated for death in battle for the common defence, than that this wholesale and unrestrained indulgence in what is called " vivisection " should be allowed to go on and to increase its needless extravagance of torture.

Your work is in behalf of men as well as of the dumb creatures of God, for no human being can practise these torments habitually without developing the latent savagery of his own nature. No zeal for science can justify it. It would be much better to dissect men alive occasionally for the general welfare, because the attendant phenomena *and demonstrations of the victims, being of our own particular form of animal, would be far more valuable than the result of our observation upon the physical structure illustrated in the agonies unto death of the helpless creatures around us.*

I hope that your pamphlet may have universal circulation. It will make us a better people.

Truly yours,
HENRY W. BLAIR.

From Senator Chandler, of New Hampshire : —

UNITED STATES SENATE,
WASHINGTON, D. C., *March 31, 1890.*

MY DEAR SIR :

Yours of March 28th, with your pamphlet, is at hand. You are doing a noble work with conciseness, decision, and courage.

I cannot believe it possible that the interests of medical science require the vivisection of animals.

Yours truly,

WM. E. CHANDLER.

PHILIP G. PEABODY, Esq.

From Rev. Dr. Morgan Dix, Rector of Trinity Parish, New York : —

NEW YORK, *April 1st, 1890.*

PHILIP G. PEABODY, Esq.,
Attorney and Counsellor-at-Law,
18 Richfield Street, Boston :

My dear Sir, — I acknowledge receipt of your communication of the 20th ulto., together with a copy of your pamphlet entitled *Vivisection in America.* You request me to read that pamphlet. I respectfully decline to do so, as the subject is too horrible for consideration. I have read accounts of the tortures inflicted in the name of Science on the creatures committed to our care or placed in our power by a Divine Providence, and they have made me sick at heart for weeks together. I shall never peruse these frightful statistics again. I have also read what arguments are made in extenuation or recommendation of the practice, and their only effect has been to strengthen my conviction that man is capable of becoming the most barbarous and most merciless of all agents.

I gladly join with any one who protests against the abuse of our power over confiding and intelligent animals.

The lower creation is a deep mystery. There are in it intelligent and sensitive beings with virtues which man may well imitate, and with qualities which inspire affection. God has given us dominion over them and powers which we ought not to abuse ; and when I go into His presence I wish to be able to tell Him that I abhor, detest, and protest against the tortures of these poor creatures under the pretence of thereby benefiting our own lordly race.

You may make what use you please of this letter.

I remain, in conclusion,

Respectfully yours,

MORGAN DIX.

From Mr. Denman Thompson :—

NEW YORK, *April 1, 1890.*

MY DEAR MR. PEABODY :

I heartily endorse the sentiments against the horrors of vivisection expressed in the pamphlet on *Vivisection in America*, which you were kind enough to send me. Cruelty to dumb animals is wrong in itself, and the most elaborate scientific plea cannot justify it. I have always been an advocate of scientific progress, but I cannot bring myself to believe in the utility of torturing — in the name of medical science — animals who cannot protest for themselves.

Very truly,

DENMAN THOMPSON.

From Senator Dolph, of Oregon :—

UNITED STATES SENATE,
WASHINGTON, D. C., *April 3d, 1890.*

PHILIP G. PEABODY, Esq.,
18 Richfield St., Boston, Mass.

Dear Sir, — I am just in receipt of your favor of the 31st ult.

Also a copy of your pamphlet entitled *Vivisection in America*, which I have read with interest.

I heartily approve of its purposes, and sympathize with you in the good work you have undertaken.

Yours truly,

J. N. DOLPH.

From Rev. Dr. C. A. Bartol, of Boston :—

HOTEL DEL CORONADO, E. S. BABCOCK, Jr., Manager,
CORONADO, CALIF., *1st April, 1890.*

DEAR FRIEND :

I should only repeat your views in expressing my own. Animals, being our relations, have rights which we are bound to respect.

God speed your cause,

C. A. BARTOL.

From Dr. Edward Berdoe, of England : —

TYNEMOUTH HOUSE, VICTORIA PARK GATE, N. E.,
LONDON, *1st April, 1890.*

MY DEAR SIR :

I have carefully read the pamphlet which you were good enough to send me, entitled *Vivisection in America.* There is not a statement therein which I cannot heartily endorse. So far from there being the slightest exaggeration, I can testify from my own knowledge that the atrocious cruelties which you condemn are daily and hourly performed in the physiological laboratories of the world. I do not speak rashly, for I have labored for the past ten years in combating the practices of vivisection in England, and have made it my business to ascertain precisely what is being carried on in medical schools and universities, in the name of the healing art, in America. It seems to me that you can hardly be engaged in a nobler work than in protesting against this great wrong. It strikes a blow at our common humanity, and if tolerated by society will inevitably be fatal to its highest interests.

I am, my dear Sir,
Yours very faithfully,
EDWARD BERDOE,
Member of the Royal College of Surgeons of England: Licentiate of the Royal College of Edinburgh; Member of the British Medical Association, etc., etc.

Extracts from a personal letter from Miss Frances Power Cobbe, author of "The Scientific Spirit of the Age," "The Hopes of the Human Race," "The Peak in Darien," "Alone to the Alone," "False Beasts and True," "The Duties of Woman:" —

HENGWRT, DOLGELLY, N. WALES, *April 6.*

MY DEAR MR. PEABODY :

I have received the copy of *Vivisection in America* which you have kindly sent me, and am delighted with the handsome reprint. Your introductory letter also is excellent and gives the paper a good American *imprimatur.* I owe you hearty and grateful thanks for your powerful co-operation in this hard fight.

You will probably have seen the long report in the *Worcester Sunday Telegram*, of March 9, of the vivisection going on upon a frightful scale at Clark University. The fact to which I wish specially to direct your attention, if by chance you have not seen the paper, is that the poor, wretched dogs to be vivisected are regularly sent to this university *from Boston.* It seems to me possible that you may be able in Boston to look into this abominable trade.

Ever yours most truly,

FRANCES POWER COBBE.

From "Ouida : " —

4th April, 1890.

MR. PHILIP G. PEABODY :

Dear Sir, — You cannot feel more deeply than I do the horrors of the sacrifices made to so-called science. Were the public everywhere not so apathetic, so selfish, and so ignorant as is unhappily the bulk of every nation, vivisection and all its congeners would be made impossible. The frightful experiments, frequently lasting for months on the same creature, are wholly unknown to the chief part of the world, whilst most of those to whom they are known are afraid to seem "behind the age" if they oppose them, or turn their eyes away from what pains and distresses them, stupidly accepting the bland lies of physiologists. Physiology has become a trade — a lucrative pursuit. So long as the nations provide laboratories and salaries, so long will needy men climb by it into comfortable college chairs. The immense difficulty in our way is, 1st, the egotism of human nature, delighted to hope that disease may be banished and death deferred by some discovery ; 2d, the dense apathy of it before all pain not inflicted upon itself. If you have in your city the back volumes of the *Gentlemen's Magazine* you will find an article of mine on vivisection. I forget the year, but think it was '82 or '83. Pray make any use of this letter that you choose, and attach my name to any declaration against scientific torture.

Please address only, " Mme. Ouida, Florence."

Obediently yours,

OUIDA.

From Baron von Weber, of Germany, Knight of the Royal Order of Saxony, etc.; President of the Great German League against Scientific Cruelty ; Honorary Corresponding Member of the Society for the Protection of Animals from Vivisection : —

DRESDEN, *13th April, 1890.*

DEAR SIR :

I have read with great interest the valuable book you sent me, and I wish that you may be able to give it a large circulation between the Atlantic and the Pacific ; then it may be hoped that it shall awake the consciences of many honest people in the United States, and that numerous friends of true humanity will unite to put a stop to the abominable cruelties in the vivisectionist laboratories.

I remain, dear Sir,

Faithfully yours,

ERNST VON WEBER.

From Miss Fanny Davenport : —

BRUNSWICK, BOSTON.

TO PHILIP G. PEABODY.

My dear Sir,—Much as I wish to write at length on the subject of your pamphlet, I regret I have not the time to spare. However, these few words I will write, hoping they may in a small degree express the feelings I have upon the matter. Cruelty, to my mind, is as black a sin as any other sin so named, and that human creatures can inflict upon the helpless (those creatures sent by God for our use, our comfort, and our needs) such intentional pain, seems almost the capability of a brute. To me those who practise vivisection are no higher in their natures than the brute whom they make to suffer — a poor creature without the means of resenting, that cannot speak and cry for mercy, but whose sufferings must be as great as any mortal's. In my humble opinion, such practice should be a punishable offence, and I for one am with "The Society" heart and soul in its object, and if I can in any way further the good work, command me.

Faithfully yours,

FANNY DAVENPORT.

From Col. Robert G. Ingersoll : —

LAW OFFICE,
ROBERT G. INGERSOLL, 45 WALL STREET,
NEW YORK, *May 27, 1890.*

PHILIP G. PEABODY, Esq. :

Boston, Mass.

My dear Friend, — Vivisection is the Inquisition — the Hell — of Science. All the cruelty which the human — or rather the inhuman — heart is capable of inflicting, is in this one word. Below this there is no depth. This word lies like a coiled serpent at the bottom of the abyss.

We can excuse, in part, the crimes of passion. We take into consideration the fact that man is liable to be caught by the whirlwind, and that from a brain on fire the soul rushes to a crime. But what excuse can ingenuity form for a man who deliberately — with an unaccelerated pulse — with the calmness of John Calvin at the murder of Servetus — seeks, with curious and cunning knives, in the living, quivering flesh of a dog, for all the throbbing nerves of pain? The wretches who commit these infamous crimes pretend that they are working for the good of man ; that they are actuated by philanthropy ; and that their pity for the sufferings of the human race drives out all pity for the animals they slowly torture to death. But those who are incapable of pitying animals are, as a matter of fact, incapable of pitying men. A physician who would cut a living rabbit in pieces — laying bare the nerves, denuding them with knives, pulling them out with forceps — would not hesitate to try experiments with men and women for the gratification of his curiosity.

To settle some theory, he would trifle with the life of any patient in his power. By the same reasoning he will justify the vivisection of animals and patients. He will say that it is better that a few animals should suffer than that one human being should die ; and that it is far better that one patient should die, if through the sacrifice of that one, several may be saved.

Brain without heart is far more dangerous than heart without brain.

Have these scientific assassins discovered anything of value ? They may have settled some disputes as to the action of some organ, but have they added to the useful knowledge of the race?

It is not necessary for a man to be a specialist in order to have and express his opinion as to the right or wrong of vivisection. It is not necessary to be a scientist or a naturalist to detest cruelty and to love mercy. Above all the discoveries of the thinkers, above all the inventions of the ingenious, above all the victories won on fields of intellectual conflict, rise human sympathy and a sense of justice.

I know that good for the human race can never be accomplished by torture. I also know that all that has been ascertained by vivisection could have been done by the dissection of the dead, or at least of animals completely and perfectly under the merciful influence of ether. I know that all the torture has been useless. All the agony inflicted has simply hardened the hearts of the criminals, without enlightening their minds.

It may be that the human race might be physically improved if all the sickly and deformed babes were killed, and if all the paupers, liars, drunkards, thieves, villains, and vivisectionists were murdered. All this might, in a few ages, result in the production of a generation of physically perfect men and women ; but what would such beings be worth, — men and women healthy and heartless, muscular and cruel — that is to say, intelligent wild beasts?

Never can I be the friend of one who vivisects his fellow-creatures. I do not wish to touch his hand.

When the angel of pity is driven from the heart; when

the fountain of tears is dry, — the soul becomes a serpent crawling in the dust of a desert.

Thanking you for the good you are doing, and wishing you the greatest success, I remain,

Yours always,

R. G. INGERSOLL.

Courteous replies have also been received from United States Senator Plumb, Mr. Charles Dudley Warner, Mr. Herbert Spencer (of England), Mr. George Kennan, United States Senator Allison, Rev. O. B. Frothingham, Mr. James Parton, Hon. Robert C. Winthrop, Ex-Attorney-General and Judge Devens, Rev. Andrew P. Peabody, Hon. Henry Cabot Lodge, United States Senator Ingalls, Gen. and Ex-Gov. Benjamin F. Butler, and a large number of others, of which those printed above were all that the undersigned considered advisable to publish with this edition of the pamphlet. Most of those not printed express the warmest sympathy for the Anti-Vivisection cause, but the writers of some of them found it impossible, through extreme preoccupation of time, or from other causes, to comply with the request for written expressions of their sentiments for publication.

PHILIP G. PEABODY.

It is intended that all profits accruing from the sale of this work shall be donated to one of the Anti-Vivisection societies, or divided between a number of them.

It is requested that all persons, in any part of the United States, who are willing to give either labor, money, or the influence of their names toward the *absolute prohibition* of Vivisection, will send their names and addresses to the undersigned.

PHILIP G. PEABODY,

BOSTON, MASS.

VIVISECTION IN AMERICA.

THAT Vivisection on a considerable scale is practised in the United States is a fact which has been denied by men otherwise well and widely informed respecting American affairs. Great cruelties, it has been generally confessed, have been committed on the continent of Europe, notably in Germany, France, and Italy; but English-speaking nations have been credited with a degree of humane feeling extending even to this method of research,—"naturally liable," as the Royal Commission reported, "to great abuse;"—and it is commonly believed that neither in Great Britain nor the United States has anything approaching to the recklessness of continental Vivisection been exhibited.

For the truth, as regards England, of this nationally-flattering view of the matter, the reader is referred to Dr. Berdoe's recent pamphlet, *Twelve Years' Trial of the Vivisection Act.* It will be found therein proved that "under all the so-called restrictions of the present Act, the most terrible cruelties are daily and hourly practised (in England); and that iniquities only equalled by those

---

* *Twelve Years' Trial of the Vivisection Act.* By M.R.C.S. London and New York: Swan, Sonnenschein. Price 3d.

which are admitted to be horrible when done abroad, are regularly performed in our great Universities and Schools of Medicine."

As regards America, we propose in the following pages to marshal for the Reader's judgment extracts from the writings of American physiologists, illustrating the actual character and extent of Vivisection in the United States during the present decade. We shall divide our extracts into,

1st, those concerned with the Teaching of Vivisection to students;

2nd, those recording the Practice of American physiologists.

I.—TEACHING VIVISECTION.

DR. AUSTIN FLINT was one of the most eminent Profes-
sors of Physiology in America, and was welcomed as such
in London at the International Medical Congress of 1881.
He was Professor of Physiology and Microscopy at the
Bellevue Medical College, New York, and at Long Island
College Hospital. In his Preface to the Third Edition of
his great work, the *Physiology of Man*,* he was able to con-
gratulate himself on the success it had achieved. His aim
had been to write "a book which would meet the wants of
practitioners and students of Medicine;" and he says:
"My expectations in this regard have been more than ful-
filled. My work has been very favorably received by the
profession : it is extensively used as a text-book, and two
large impressions of the first edition, and a second edition
published in 1874, have been exhausted."

We may thus safely proceed to scan Professor Flint's
observations and avowals as having all been most "favorably received" by the medical profession in America ;—
received, it must be noted, with so complete an absence of
reserve on account of the severity of the experiments it

---

* Five vols. New York. Appleton & Co. This book has
been subsequently condensed into one volume.

details and recommends, that it has been "extensively used as a text-book" for the instruction of the rising generation of American doctors.

What, then, were Dr. Austin Flint's views and practice respecting training in Vivisection?

In the preface to the earlier editions of his *Physiology of Man*, p. 8, he says :—

"For some years the author has been in the habit of employing vivisection in public teachings." Again, in the same work, Vol. II., p. 300, in speaking of a frightful experiment in which an animal was caused to vomit from a pig's bladder, which had been substituted for a stomach, he says, "These experiments were made simply for demonstrations."

In his Report to the Medical Congress, 1881, he refers to several other experiments used for demonstration : "We have long been in the habit in class demonstrations of removing the optic lobe on one side from a pigeon," &c., &c.

With these views of the propriety of demonstrations to students, it is not surprising that Dr. Flint's Text-book should bristle at every page with records of vivisections, often of the most agonizing kind, performed by dead and living physiologists all over the world, and cited as "interesting" or instructive, but never, (as may be imagined,) with a word of condemnation or of caution as to their repetition. Indeed, as to repeating experiments perpetually, he himself avows in the above quoted *Report:* "Our own experiments, which have been very numerous during the last fifteen years, are simply repetitions of Flourens, and the results have been the same without exception."

Accordingly we find in the *Physiology of Man* * such

---

* One vol. New York. Appleton. 3rd Ed., 1884.

experiments as the following. Chauveau's experiments
(most *interesting* as usual!) and Faivre's on the hearts of
monkeys, p. 45. Marey's experiment of thrusting a sound
into the heart of a horse through the jugular vein, p. 44.
Rouanet's and the British Commission's experiments on
the sounds of the heart, wherein "the semi-lunar valves
were caught up by curved hooks introduced through the
vessels of an ass," p. 47. Legallois', Brachet's and Bernard's experiments on the influence of the nervous system
on the heart, p. 58-9. Erichsen's and Schiff's demonstration of causes of arrest of action of the heart, p. 62.
Hale's and Bernard's experiments in blood pressure on
the carotid of the horse, p. 78. Cyon and Ludwig on the
results of division of the splanchnic nerves of rabbits, p.
79. Majendie, p. 101, and His, Robin, Hertz, and others,
p. 107, contribute other observations on the circulation.
We are told that the epiglottis has been frequently removed from the lower animals by Majendie and his follow-
ers, p. 117; but, on this point, Flint thinks (wonderful to
relate!) that it "becomes a question whether the experiment (the ablation of the epiglottis) can be absolutely
applied to the human subject." The chapter on Respiration is a series of such citations of experiments by Majendie, Bernard, Allen, Pepys, Regnault, Reinet, Legallois,
&c. The same may be said of Chapter VI. on Alimenta-
tion (where starvation of animals comes into play) and of
that on Digestion, where, however, we light on the candid
admission that "Taking only into consideration experiments
upon the inferior animals, little definite information has
been obtained concerning the composition and properties
of the intestinal juice," p. 266. A dog with a pancreatic
fistula, artificially induced, is shown at p. 271. Another
dog, with biliary fistula, artificially induced, and muzzled to
prevent him licking himself, is shown at p. 282, and it is
observed that he "is considerably emaciated." On the

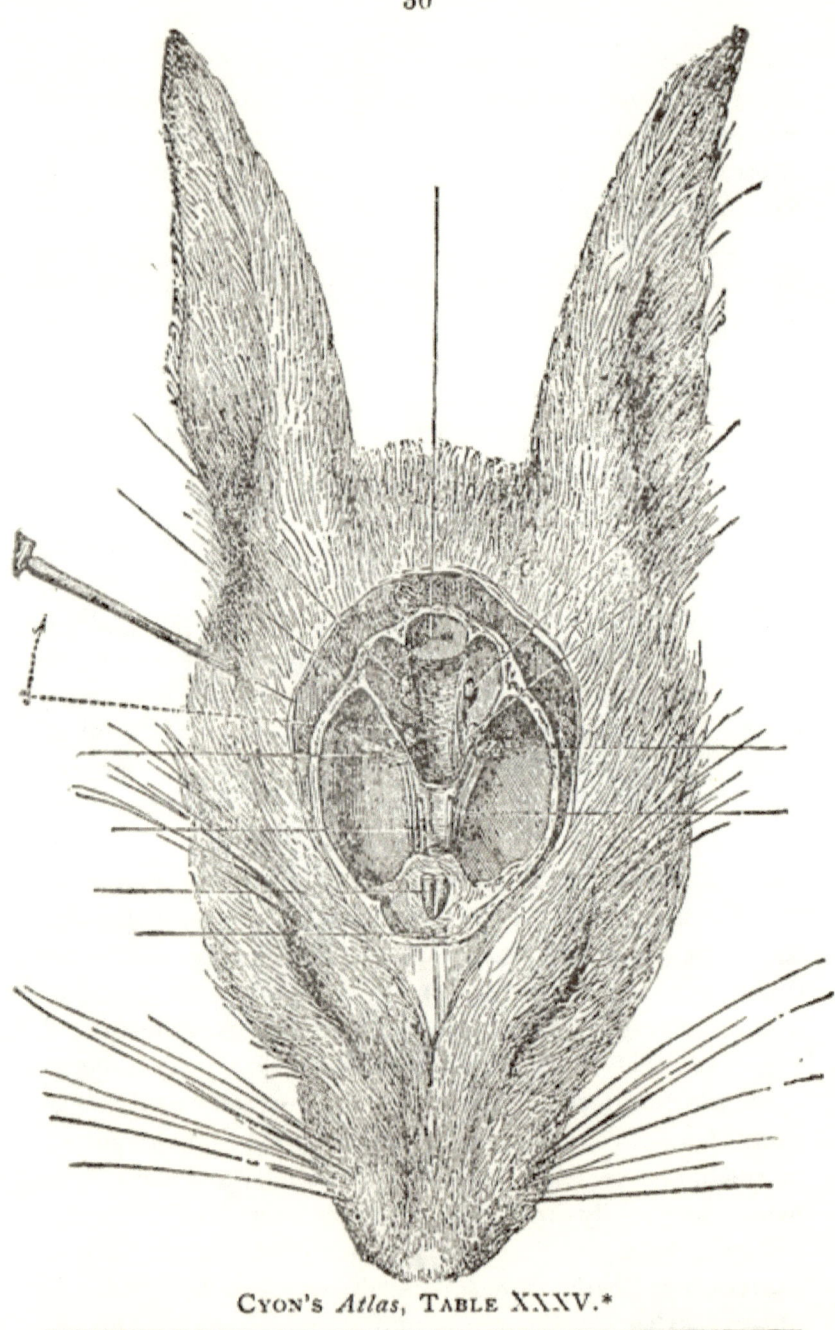

CYON'S *Atlas*, TABLE XXXV.*

*NOTE.—The above figure shows the head of a dead rabbit,

subject of "Absorption" the experiments of Prévost and Dumas (p. 317), and Bernard (p. 318) are quoted. Also those of Lebkúchner and Majendie (p. 321), of Dutrochet (pp. 321-2), of Matteucci, Longet, Milne-Edwards, Von Becker (pp. 326-7), and many others. And so on throughout ; experiments on the kidneys, the liver, the spleen, and other organs being constantly cited as the basis or support of knowledge on the subject thereof. And similarly with the nervous and cerebral systems.

At page 640 is reproduced the figure from Cyon's *Atlas* to illustrate, on the head of a rabbit, the operation for division of the fifth nerve—an experiment which Cyon states always causes a cry of agony from the unfortunate animal. On the page preceding (639) is shown the "instrument for dividing the fifth nerve" (after Bernard). At page 727 is shown the form of a "Stylet for breaking up the medulla oblongata" (after Bernard).

In short, the whole of Professor Flint's treatise may be taken as a rehearsal and description of the worst vivisections

---

of which the brain and top of the skull is removed to show the position of the nerves, and the instrument is exhibited piercing the head (as in life), and reaching the nerves (the trigeminus) on which it is desired to operate. The description given by Cyon of the method of this operation (*Methodik*, p. 512) is as follows : "The rabbit is firmly fastened to the ordinary vivisecting table by means of Czermak's holder. Then the rabbit's head is held by the left hand, so that the thumb of that hand rests on the condyle of the lower jaw. This is used as a *point d'appui* for the insertion of the knife. . . . .To reach the hollow of the temple the instrument must be guided forward and upward, thus avoiding the hard portion of the temporal bone and leading the knife directly into the cranial cavity. . . . .The trigeminus then comes under the knife. Now holding the head of the animal very firmly, the blade of the knife is directed backwards and downwards and pressed hard in this direction against the base of the skull. The nerve is then generally cut behind the Gasserian ganglion, which is announced by a violent cry of agony *(einen heftigen Schmerzensschrei)* of the animal."

of French, German, and Italian physiologists,—all detailed
for the instruction, and (we can scarcely question, seeing
that not a breath of blame attaches to any of them), for the
emulation of American youth.

But all these examples quoted by Professor Flint, evil as
they are, appear to be outdone by experiments which he
himself performed as demonstrations to his students. The
following account is extracted from the well-known article
by Dr. Albert Leffingwell in *Lippincott's Magazine*, August,
1884 :—

"There is a certain experiment, one of the most excruciating which can be performed, which consists in exposing
the spinal cord of the dog for the purpose of demonstrating
the function of the spinal nerves. . . . . It is not the
cutting operation which forms its chief peculiarity or to
which special objection would be made. At present all this
preliminary process is generally performed under anæsthetics. It is an hour or two later, when the animal has partly
recovered from the severe shock of the operation, that the
wound is re-opened and the experiment begins. It was
during a class demonstration of this kind by Majendie,
before the introduction of ether, that the circumstance
occurred which one hesitates to think possible in a person
retaining a single spark of humanity or pity. 'I recall to
mind,' says Dr. Latour, who was present at the time, 'a
poor dog, the roots of whose vertebral nerves Majendie desired to lay bare to demonstrate Bell's theory, which he
claimed as his own. The dog, mutilated and bleeding,
twice escaped from under the implacable knife, and threw
its front paws around Majendie's heel, licking as if to soften
his murderer and ask for pity. I confess I was unable to
endure that heart-rending spectacle.'"

[After quoting the evidence of Ferrier, Pavy, Gull, and
Michael Foster before the English Royal Commission of
1875—to prove that English students would "rebel" at the

sight of such an experiment, and that no leading man in Germany would exhibit anything of the kind,—Dr. Leffing-well continues with reference to America] : (Italics ours.)

"Now mark the contrast. This experiment—which we are told passes even the callousness of Germany to repeat ; which every leading champion of vivisection in Great Britain reprobates for medical teaching ; which some of them shrink even from seeing, themselves, from horror at the tortures necessarily inflicted ; which the most ruthless among them *dare not* exhibit to the young men of England,—THIS *experiment has been performed publicly again and again in American medical colleges*, without exciting, so far as we know, even a whisper of protest or the faintest murmur of remonstrance ! The proof is to be found in the published statements of the experimenter himself. In his *Text-book of Physiology*, Professor Flint says, 'Majendie . . . . showed very satisfactorily that the posterior roots (of the spinal cord) were exclusively sensory, and this fact has been con-firmed by more recent observations upon the higher classes of animals. We have ourselves *frequently* exposed and irritated the roots of the nerves in dogs, *in public demon-strations* in experiments on the recurrent sensibility, ... and in another series of observations.' "

"This is the experience of a single professional teacher ; but it is improbable that this experiment has been shown only to the students of a single medical college in the United States ; it has doubtless been repeated again and again in different colleges throughout the country. If Englishmen are, then, so extremely sensitive as Ferrier, Gull, and Burdon-Sanderson would have us believe, we must neces-sarily conclude that the sentiment of compassion is far greater in Britain than in America. Have we drifted back-ward in humanity ? Have American students learned to witness, without protest, tortures at the sight of which

English students would rebel?"—*Lippincott's Magazine*, August, 1884, p. 130.)

In the face of these facts, and of the position held by Dr. Austin Flint as the author of the accepted American Text-Book of Physiological instruction, we are driven to the mournful conclusion that, as regards the *Teaching* of Vivisection, America stands even lower than England; lower, possibly, than Germany itself.

II.—PRACTICE.

We now turn to the Practice of Vivisection during the last decade in America; and to study this we shall cite the published Reports of their experiments by the Vivisectors themselves, as they stand in some of the leading scientific periodicals of the United States and in those of England to which American Physiologists have been contributors.

Here is a series of examples from the *Journal of Physiology.*[*]

Vol. I., pp. 193-5, 1879-80, Dr. Isaac Ott, Lecturer on Experimental Physiology, University of Pennsylvania, and G. B. Woodfield, Student of medicine, published a paper on "Sweat Centres; the Effect of Muscarin and Atropin on Them." The article commences thus :—

"The fact that, besides sensory and motor nerves, secretory nerves exist, was established by the brilliant experiments of Ludwig on the submaxillary gland,—although the theory of excito-secretory function was put forth by Campbell, of Georgia. Goltz was the first to notice that after irritation of a nerve the sweat secretion was increased.

---

[*] The *Journal of Physiology* is published at Cambridge (England), and its Editor-in-chief is Dr. Michael Foster, Professor of Physiology in the University, and Secretary of the Royal Society, London, who may be considered the head centre of Vivisection in England. There are associated with Professor Foster in the Editorship, Professor H. P. Bowditch, of Boston; Professor H. Newell Martin, of Baltimore; Professor H. C. Wood, of Philadelphia. The *Journal* may therefore be deemed to be the medium of intercommunication between England and America among physiologists.

Luchsinger, of Zurich, and Miss Kendall, of Boston, found that after irritation of the sciatic or bronchial nerves in the dog or cat, an increased secretion of sweat took place, and that it ensued after ligature of the aorta, and during the first fifteen minutes after amputation of an extremity,"* &c.

The authors go on to state :—

"We made some experiments, of which the following are examples :—

"Experiment I. Cat placed on Czermak's holder, sciatic laid bare and irritated with Du Bois' apparatus ; an exaggerated secretion of sweat followed.

"Experiment II. Cat : Posterior extremity amputated with the sciatic attached ; when an electric current was applied to the nerve the secretion of sweat commenced."

"Experiment III. Cat placed in holder and etherised, spinal cord divided in the dorsal region, and sciatic divided on one side. On inducing asphyxia [?when the effect of the ether had disappeared] sweating took place in all the extremities excepting that which had suffered section of the sciatic."

"Experiment IV. Cat : spinal cord divided between the 8th and 9th dorsal vertebræ. On the next day the sciatic was divided, and a few drops of a solution of muscarin injected subcutaneously at 9 a.m. The muscarin used was obtained from Merck's laboratory, and given in the shape of a sulphate. 9.3 a.m., salivation and sweating of all the feet, pupil contracted ; 9.7 a.m., defæcation and labored breathing, atropin subcutaneously injected ; 9.12 a.m., sweating checked in all the extremities ; 9.16 a.m., injection of atropin repeated ; 9.28 a.m., again repeated ; 10.4 a.m., sweating and salivation nearly completely checked.

"Experiment V. Cat : spinal cord divided between the 8th and 9th dorsal vertebræ. On the third day after the

---

* Perspiration ensues upon pain ; was not this sweating so caused ?

section of the cord two drops of the muscarin solution were injected subcutaneously at 4.59 p.m. Sciatic previously divided; 5.1 p.m., sweating commencing; 5.6 p.m., all the extremities moist, salivation; 5.7 p.m., .003 grain of atropin sulphate subcutaneously; 5.10 p.m., all the feet are dry."

In the same *Journal of Physiology*, Vol. II. pp. 24, *et seq.*, is an account by H. Newell Martin, Professor of Biology in the Johns Hopkins Univ., Baltimore, U.S.A., and Edward Mussey Hartwell, M.A., of experiments "On the Respiratory Function of the Internal Intercostal Muscles," which begins by making the following remarkable admission :—

"An inspection of the ordinary text-books of physiology is sufficient to show that the part played by the internal intercostal muscles, in the production of the respiratory movements of the mammal, is still a subject upon which there is no agreement among physiologists." Reference is then made to the text-books of Dalton, Ludwig, Vierordt, Carpenter, Flint, Hermann, McKendrick, Donders, Funke, and Foster, all of whom appear to have experimented on the point, and still left it "an open question."

The authors continue : —

"Dogs and cats were employed in our experiments. The animals having been etherised, tracheotomy was performed, and the apparatus for artificial respiration connected with the windpipe.* The abdomen was opened by an incision along the *linea alba* and a transverse incision, so as to expose the diaphragm from below. The skin and the serratus and pectoral and other muscles were then dissected away from one side of the chest so as to lay bare the external intercostal muscles from the fourth or fifth to the ninth or tenth ribs: except where they were covered at their dorsal portions by the muscles running alongside the

---

* This implies the administration of curare, which would render the ether useless and needless for "keeping the animal quiet" for a short time.

vertebral column. During this operation several small vessels commonly required tying, especially in the dog.

"One intercostal space, say that between the eighth and ninth ribs, was then selected, and the anterior part of the external intercostal muscle divided, near its attachment to the lower of the two ribs, for from an inch to an inch and a half at its sternal end. The internal intercostal, which was carefully avoided during the operation, then remained alone with the pleura uniting the front part of the two ribs. The eighth and ninth costal cartilages and the tissues between them were next divided, the chest opened, and the artificial respiration apparatus set at work. The tissues in the seventh and ninth intercostal spaces were then completely divided nearly all the way back to the vertebral column.

"Next, from the pleural side, a fine-bladed knife was inserted between the eighth intercostal nerve and the eighth rib near the vertebral column and an incision carried forward, without cutting the nerve, until it reached the outer end of the region where the external intercostal muscle had been divided. . . . . An incision of similar extent was then made along the upper border of the ninth rib, and finally a bit of both ribs corresponding in extent and position to these incisions was completely cut away by bone forceps," &c. Other dissections of the parts of the living animals are described as having been carried out, and then a string was attached to a rib "and passed over a pulley to a lever which carried a weight and extended the muscle. This lever carried a pen which wrote on the paper of a Ludwig's kymographion," &c.

"The artificial respiration was then stopped, and the animal was generally found apnoeic. The further course of events differ in the dog and cat." Both, however, show "expiratory convulsions," and sometimes the artificial respiration is renewed "and the animal kept alive" for the exhibition of further phenomena.

At pages 82-90 of the same volume are recorded the results of experiments on dogs, involving vivisection, in reference to "Pharyngeal Respiration," by Dr. G. M. Garland, Assistant in Physiology at Harvard Medical School, Boston.

At pages 191-201 in the same volume is a paper "On the so-called heat dyspnœa," by Dr. Christian Sihler, Fellow of the Johns Hopkins University, Baltimore. After reciting Goldstein's experiments on the same subject, the author describes experiments made by himself. He says (p. 184) : "I have repeated all the experiments of Goldstein," and five of these are related. In Goldstein's first experiment, we are told—

"The animal (dog) is placed in a box and heated, its nose being exposed ; the frequency of the respiration increases as the temperature goes up. The animal is taken out when its temperature has reached 41·2° C." In the second experiment of Goldstein a cat was used, in the third a dog, into the veins of which morphine had been injected. The temperature was raised to 40° C. in this case, and the respirations went up from 16 to 366 per minute. In the fourth experiment the vagi were cut, and two tubes filled with hot water were applied to the carotid artery. In reference to this experiment, Dr. Sihler observes that an increase of the respirations in the animal was the result, but that it "is really, as one cannot fail to observe, brought about by pain ; for it must be remembered that water at 54°, to say nothing of 71°, is decidedly painful to the hand.* That it was pain that called forth these rapid respirations, is shown by the fact that when I let the water of the same (54°) temperature run into wounds made in the thighs, the

---

* 54 centigrade, as above, is equal to 129·2 Fahrenheit : and 71 centigrade equal to 159·8 Fahrenheit.

same increase in the respiratory rate occurred" (p. 194). Other experiments were made, each animal being under observation for about two hours.

The subject is further pursued by Dr. Sihler in the *Journal of Physiology*, Vol. III., pp. 1-10.

In the *Journal of Physiology*, Vol. III., page 76, 1880-1882, are published the experiments of William Councilman, M. D., of Johns Hopkins University. His experiments consisted in producing artificial keratitis (inflammation of the cornea) in the eyes of frogs and cats by passing a thread through the centre of the cornea and bringing it out through the sclerotic coat ; the application of various caustics, such as croton oil, nitrate of silver, caustic potassa, and the hot iron ; pricking the cornea with a needle.*

In the sixth volume of the *Journal of Physiology*, May, 1885 (pp. 133-5), is a "Note on the Nature of Nerve Force," by Dr. H. P. Bowditch, Professor of Physiology, Harvard Medical School, in which it is stated as follows :—

"The failure of Wedenskii's experiments on frogs may well be supposed to depend upon the slow and uncertain manner in which curare is eliminated by frogs.

"It seemed therefore desirable to investigate the subject upon warm-blooded animals, and the following experiment was performed :—

"A cat was etherised, and the sciatic nerve divided near the sacrum. A pair of shielded electrodes was then placed upon the same nerve lower down in the thigh. The tendon of the tibialis anticus was dissected out and connected with a lever which recorded the contraction of the muscle on the smoked paper covering a cylinder revolving once in twelve hours. The secondary coil of an ordinary induction apparatus was then connected with the electrodes, and the

---

* This information formed part of a valuable Report kindly supplied to the authors by Mrs. C. E. White, of Philadelphia.

minimum intensity of stimulation requisite to produce a
tetanic contraction of the muscle was determined . . . . .
The animal then received a dose of curare ($0.007—0.01$
grain) sufficient to prevent muscular contractions, and the
irritation of the nerve was steadily maintained while the
animal was kept alive by artificial respiration. In the
course of one and a-half to two hours the curare was so far
eliminated that the stimulation of the nerve, which previously had been without effect, began to produce muscular
twitches which, as the elimination of the drug progressed,
became more frequent and more violent. A true tetanus,
however, was never observed.

"In some experiments a second dose of curare was given,
when the muscle began to twitch and the experiment was
continued till the drug was a second time eliminated. In
this way it was found that stimulation of the nerve lasting from one and a-half to four hours (the muscle being
prevented from contracting by curare) did not exhaust the
nerve, since on the elimination of the curare the muscle
began to contract" (pp. 134-5).

In the same volume (pp. 162-76) is a paper entitled "A
Study of the Action of the Depressor Nerve, and a Con-
sideration of the Effect of Blood-pressure upon the Heart
regarded as a Sensory Organ." By Henry Sewell, Ph. D.,
Professor of Physiology in the University of Michigan, and
D. W. Steiner, M. D., Assistant in Physiology (from the
Physiological Laboratory at Ann Arbor, Mich.) ; wherein
are described thirty severe experiments on cats and rabbits.

The seventh volume of the *Journal of Physiology* (pp.
416-50), November, 1886, contains a report of "Plethys-
mographic Experiments on the Vaso-Motor Nerves of the
Limbs," by Dr. H. P. Bowditch, Professor of Physiology,
and Dr. J. W. Warren, Assistant in Physiology, Harvard
Medical School. The following are extracts :—

"After some preliminary experiments on other animals it

was decided to employ cats in this research, since adult cats vary less than dogs in size and other physical peculiarities, and are much more vigorous and tenacious of life than rabbits or other animals usually employed in physiological laboratories. The latter point is one of considerable importance in experiments extending over several hours. . . . The animals were curarised and kept alive by artificial respiration, while the peripheric end of the divided sciatic nerve was stimulated by induction shocks varying in intensity and frequency" (p. 419,) . . . The cat to be experimented upon was etherised by being placed under a large bell-glass together with a sponge saturated with sulphuric ether, and then secured back upwards on a board of suitable size and construction, the head being held in an ordinary Czermak's rabbit-holder. The sciatic nerve was then divided as near as possible to its point of exit from the pelvis by the following operation, which is similar to that described by Cyon* for the dog.

"The skin is divided on a line drawn from the joint of the tail and the sacrum to the trochanter, care being taken not to cut too near the vertebræ on account of a large vein usually found in that region. This incision falls very near a well-defined white line of the fascia, which is then to be cut through. This line marks the division of what Mivart† calls the two parts of the gluteus maximus. The posterior portion is lifted with a blunt hook, pushed back and held there, while another hook is put under the anterior portion and the gluteus medius which lies below. These muscles being drawn forward, the nerve is brought into view, except in those cases where it is necessary to remove some adipose tissue for its exposure. The nerve may then be raised on a hook, and divided, or a portion of it excised, as the experiment may require. In some cats the nerve appears to be

---

*Methodik, p. 190.   †The Cat, p. 155.

exceedingly vascular, and the blood vessels cannot always be readily isolated, so that occasionally considerable bleeding occurs, while in other cases the nerve may be cut without losing a drop of blood.

"If the influence of nerve-degeneration on the vasomotor phenomena was to be studied, the wound was now sewed up, the cat allowed to recover from the effects of the ether, and the rest of the experiment postponed for one or more days. If the phenomena were to be studied on a freshly-divided nerve, the operation was continued," &c. (pp.425-6).

We now pass for the present from the *Journal of Physiology* to the examination of other scientific Journals.

The *Therapeutic Gazette* for July, 1885, has an article entitled, "Physiological Action of Climoline Tartrate."* The experiments were performed upon dogs, no anæsthetics having been given. In the first experiment, after having secured the dog, an incision was made to expose the submaxillary gland, so that the secretion of the gland might flow into a graduated tube, the flow being allowed to continue in this manner for a period of *ten minutes*. Two dogs were reported as having been sacrificed for this experiment. For the purpose of ascertaining its action upon the secretion of bile, *three* dogs were experimented upon, the drug being injected into the duodenum. To ascertain its action upon the spleen, two kittens were used, the drug being injected into the jugular vein. In addition, numerous dogs and cats were experimented upon for the purpose of ascertaining the influence of the drug upon Respiration, Circulation, and Elimination.

---

*The whole of these extracts from the *Therapeutic Gazette* and those that follow, down to the end of the quotation from the American Society's Fourth Report' (p. 24) are from the Report above mentioned, sent us by Mrs. C. E. White. of Philadelphia.

In the same *Gazette* for April, 1886, Dr. H. A. Hare has written an article upon "The Physiological and Therapeutical Effect of Adonidin,The Active Principle of Adonis Vernalis." In his experiments he injected the drug into the jugular vein of a number of dogs, some of them having been curarised.

Again, in the *Therapeutic Gazette* for November, 1886, are reported the experiments of Drs. Wood, Reichart, and Hare, upon *eighteen* dogs and *two* rabbits for the purpose of making observations of the action of quinine in the reduction of temperature. Artificial fever was produced by injecting pepsine into the jugular vein, and then injecting the quinine hypodermically. Some of the experiments lasted nearly eight hours, the whole time being a period of torture for the animals employed. In most of the experiments the dogs survived at least a period of twenty-four hours, but it is stated that in one case the dog was killed by pithing.

Again, in the *Therapeutic Gazette* for November, 1887, Dr. Randall Hutchinson, in "A Contribution from the Laboratory of Experimental Therapeutics of the University of Pa.," describes experiments upon frogs and dogs for the purpose of studying the action of Cimicifuga Racemosa. The extract of the drug was injected into the jugular vein of the dogs, in some cases producing death.

Again, an article in the *Therapeutic Gazette* for September, 1887, describes *twenty-six* experiments by Isaac Ott, M. D., and William S. Carter, which, undoubtedly, are of a cruel nature, and all for the useless purpose of ascertaining, if possible, "the four cerebral centres." It says: "Our experiments were performed upon rabbits, the brain being punctured through trephined openings in the skull and through the orbit. After the observations were completed the animal was killed.

When a puncture is made in the tissues between the *optic*

thalamus and the *corpus striatum* near the median line, the rabbit often utters a peculiar cry which is soon followed by increased temperature. The same experimenter, Dr. Ott, in the *Journal of Physiology*, Vol. II., p. 42, describes a number of experiments upon a number of cats—not etherised—for the purpose of making observations on the physiology of the spinal cord.

The following, (contained in the *Fourth Annual Report of the American Society for the Restriction of Vivisection, 1887,*) may also be here quoted to show to what extent private experimentation is carried on in America, albeit very little of it is brought to the knowledge of the public :—

"Dr. B. A. Watson, a prominent physician of Jersey City, was arraigned for cruelty to dogs. After having etherised the dog he would hoist it up to the ceiling and allow it to fall upon its back upon bars of iron in such a manner as to produce concussion of the spine. Some of the dogs recovered, whilst others lived from a week to ten days after the operation."

The intense suffering produced by such savage cruelty can easily be imagined.

Again, to return to the *Journal of Physiology*, in Vol. III., Dr. Isaac Ott, late Lecturer on Experimental Physiology, Univ. of Pennsylvania, has (pp. 163-4) some "Notes on Inhibition." Here "cats were selected, bound down on Czermak's holder, etherised, tracheotomy performed, the skull in the parietal region at its posterior part trephined, and the opening enlarged by the bone forceps. Artificial respiration was then set up, and a spear-shaped knife used to sever the corpora quadrigemina, thalami optici, and cerebral crura."

In the *International Journal of the Medical Sciences*, edited by I. Minis Hays, A. M., M. D., Philadelphia, and Malcolm Morris, London (Quarterly), July, 1886, we find a paper on "The Surgery of the Pancreas, as Based upon

Experiments and Clinical Researches." By N. Senn, M.D., Surgeon to the Milwaukee Hospital, Professor of Surgery in the College of Physicians and Surgeons, Chicago. We quote the following :—

"Dogs and cats were used exclusively as objects of these experiments, as a few trials soon satisfied me that in the smaller herbivora, as the rabbit and sheep, the pancreas was proportionately small and difficult of access" (p. 142).

The first two experiments were for "complete section of the pancreas." In one a dog, 35 lbs. weight, was used. The operation was performed on August 23rd, 1885, and the dog was kept alive till the 6th of December following, when he was killed, that the appearances might be examined. In the second experiment the animal was "an adult dog, medium size" (p. 143).

"Laceration of the pancreas."—Experiment on a "large adult cat, weight 7½ lbs. Abdomen opened through the median line, the pancreas exposed and detached sufficiently from the duodenum at the junction of the middle with the duodenal end, where it was torn completely across and the bleeding ends dropped into the abdominal cavity. The wound was closed in the usual manner" (p. 144). "October 17th, the wound was opened and it was reported that one end of the pancreas had protruded from the wound. The prolapsed vicus and wound were disinfected, the organ replaced, and the wound closed with sutures. The animal did not appear to be very ill, but died two days later. . . . . A portion of the duodenum appeared gangrenous" (p. 145).

Experiments were also performed involving "comminution of the pancreas," and "complete extirpation of the pancreas." One of these latter—experiment 6—was on a "brown dog, four and a-half months old; weight 32 lbs. The entire pancreas was extirpated; part of the dissection was made with Paquelin's cautery. . . . . On the fourth

day diarrhœa set in ; stools contained undigested food and
free fat, and on the seventh day blood. On the ninth day
the animal died," &c. (p. 148).

"Experiment VII. Large black dog, four months old ;
weight 48 pounds. Experience had proved that the separa-
tion of the pancreas and its vessels from the duodenum
could be done more safely, and with less risk of hemorrhage,
by tearing the tissues instead of using the scissors or knife,
employing the cutting instruments only when it was thought
imprudent to use too much violence in separating strong
connecting bands which would not yield to gentle force.
In this case twelve ligatures were required to arrest the
hemorrhage. . . . . This dog never recovered fully from
the operation, and died on the fourth day. . . . . Recent
peritonitis . . . . gangrene" (p. 148).

In Experiment VIII., the animal, a "large adult cat,"
"never rallied from the operation, and died five hours later
with symptoms of hemorrhage and shock combined." An
"adult female cat," used in Experiment IX., met its death
from similar causes, following on the extirpation of the
pancreas. In Experiment X. an "adult black dog, weight
33 pounds," was dealt with, and died of peritonitis the
fourth day after the operation. A "medium-sized adult
cat" was used in Experiment XI. "After the extirpation
of the entire pancreas, the duodenum was found on measure-
ment to have been denuded of its mesenteric attachment
to the extent of seven inches. . . . . The animal never
rallied from the operation and died two hours later."
(pp. 148-9).

Four other experiments for the "partial extirpation of the
pancreas" are recorded—two on dogs and two on cats. At
the end of four weeks the dogs became emaciated, and
after seventy-six days died of marasmus. One cat died
two days after the experimental vivisection, of "gangrene
and perforation of the duodenum," and the other died

eighteen hours after the vivisection "in convulsions." Fourteen other animals—seven dogs and seven cats—were experimented on for "Obliteration of the pancreatic duct by elastic constriction." These are recorded in detail on pages 155-57. Of the first twelve we learn that "only two of the animals recovered after isolation and double ligation of the pancreas." The other two, a "large adult cat" and a "large Newfoundland dog" were killed some time after the operation.

Four other experiments were made with "external pancreatic fistula," and eleven more with "internal pancreatic fistula." The total number of the experiments recorded is forty-three.

In the same publication, No. CLXXXIII., *New Series*, pp. 423-54, October, 1886, Dr. Senn relates forty-two cases of injury to the pancreas in the human subject in which the consequences of lesions in that organ have been studied ; these, apparently, showing the needlessness of experiments on animals.

A paper on "An experimental Research into Rabies," by Harold C. Ernst, A. M., M. D. Harv., Demonstrator of Bacteriology in the Medical School of Harvard University, is printed in the *International Journal of the Medical Sciences*, April, 1887. It contains an account of a repetition of Pasteur's experiments with rabies.

The author records that on the 2nd of July, 1886, he "received from Dr. Hamilton Osgood two rabbits, one of which had been inoculated upon the 19th or 20th of June, in Pasteur's laboratory, and had died on the 28th of June, and been kept upon ice since that time ; the second of which was inoculated on the 21st of June in Pasteur's laboratory by Pasteur himself, and, alive when received, died on the night of July 4th." With matter from the spinal cord of these Dr. Ernst inoculated by trephining thirty-two rabbits, all of which subsequently died of rabies. The symptoms

described are, first unsteadiness of gait, next stiffness or
lameness, or paralysis, then, "occasionally a decided
change in the character of the animal; from being lively
and affectionate it becomes dull and sluggish, and even
fierce—if such a term may be applied to a rabbit ; in the
latter case it will jump at and bite objects held towards it,
and may even growl and spit at them, showing every evidence
of a desire to do harm. . . . The power of deglutition
is lost in twenty-four or more hours from the first appear-
ance of any symptoms—and it was at one time supposed
that death was caused by starvation. This can hardly be
the case, however, inasmuch as the stomach is always full
of partially digested food, &c. . . . . Just before death
there seems to be a revival of the powers—as manifested
by a renewal of struggles"—to walk about, &c. Eight
other rabbits were inoculated, but owing to various causes
no result was produced. Ten more were used for "control"
experiments. Twelve guinea-pigs, nine dogs, and numerous
rabbits were used for further experiments.

In another paper in the same *Journal* Dr. Beyer, Passed
Assist.-Surg. U. S. N., describes "The Direct Action of
Atropine, Hematropine, Hyoscine, Hyoscyamine, and Da-
turine on the heart of the Dog, Terrapin, Frog."

At page 370 the author says :—

"The animal having been placed under the influence of
morphia, is fastened to a dog-holder, tracheotomy is performed, and a cannula introduced into the trachea. The
external jugular vein is then dissected out and a cannula
filled with normal salt solution introduced with its open end
pointing towards the heart. Through the latter cannula
about half-a-drachm of a one per cent. solution of curare is
injected, after which injection artificial respiration is commenced. The vagi are now found and carefully divided.
Cannulas are introduced into the cardiac end of both common carotids, the arteries being clamped on the cardiac

sides of the cannula. The first two pairs of costal cartilages are now cut away, together with the small piece of sternum which they embrace. Then the two internal mammary arteries are ligated just as they pass forward from the subclavians towards the breast bone. The whole front and sides of the thorax are now cut away, and the right subclavian artery dissected out and tied," &c. The left side of the chest is treated in much the same way. The mutilated animal, on the holder, is subsequently placed in a warm chamber, and later observations begin. The experiments are stated to have been made in May, 1886. The 21st, 26th, and 27th, were each on a "small adult dog." Eight other experiments were also made on dogs. The author refers to Ludwig's and Gaskell's experiments in a like direction, and it is clear there is only one world of physiology, which includes America along with Germany and Great Britain.

In the *International Journal of the Medical Sciences*, No. CLXXXII., October, 1887, p. 436, etc.

Dr. W. S. Halsted, of New York, relates "An Experimental Study" on "Circular Suture of the Intestine."

"Experiment A.—Small young dog. Operated on January 18th, 1887. Needles with *dulled ends* employed for sewing. Circular resection of intestine. Two rows of interrupted stitches passed as deep as, but not including any portion of submucosa—suture of muscular coat. The stitches tore badly (particularly those of the first row) and had to be frequently retaken.

"January 23rd. Dog found dead. *Autopsy:* suppurative peritonitis; sutures had given way completely."

"Experiment B.—Medium-sized dog. Operation January 18th, 1887. To include in each stitch a thread of submucosa. Irrigation with solution of corrosive sublimate, 1 : 1000. Glass clamps; suture, catgut. Two rows of interrupted stitches." The dog was killed on the 19th of February.

"Experiment C.—Operation January 20th, 1887. To reverse about one foot of intestine. . . . The "dog died of shock a few hours after operation," &c.

"To satisfy my curiosity, I made experiments D., E., and F."

Experiment D. was on a small brindled and white bull-dog (pup). Found dead the day after the operation. "Autopsy : Complete slough of flaps and gaping of circular wound."

Experiment E. was on a "large long-haired dog." This animal died on the 11th day after the operation. . . . . The experiment necessitated a good deal of stitching. It died of gangrene.

Eight experiments were performed on dogs with " Lembert's stitches." No. 1, "evidently dying of starva-tion," was killed. No. 2 was "not lively after operation," and was killed on the twelfth day following. When examined it presented abnormal and diseased conditions, the result of the experiment. Nos. 3, 4, and 5 all "died within two or three days of the operation, from purulent peritonitis."* No. 6 died under the operation, which was carried on for two hours, on a "young, small brindled dog." No. 7 was found dead two days after the operation connected with the experiment "to isolate loop" had been performed upon it. No. 8, a "rather large black and white dog," was sub-jected to experiment on January 8th, 1887, also "to isolate loop of intestine." On the 9th it was "evidently starving to death." Its abdomen was re-opened and "many and very strong adhesions" † were found to have resulted from the treatment it had been subjected to.

In another group fifteen dogs were dealt with, some of

---

* An agonising disease.

† The consequences of inflammation.

which died from the effects of the experiment, and others were killed when they appeared to be dying of starvation, being weak and emaciated." In Group III. six dogs, and in Group IV. three dogs, were utilised, all of them suffering severely, and most dying from the effects of the treatment involved in the author's experiments.

Dr. Halsted, just before summarising the results of his experiments, observes (p. 460)—

"I shall not record the rest of my experiments on circular suture of the intestine, because most of them *seem now rather absurd to me*, and none of them admit of classification."

With this significant confession we shall conclude our catalogue of cruelties committed in America by American physiologists. It will be noted,

1st, That it has been compiled almost exclusively of experiments on the higher and more sensitive animals;

2nd, That the use of curare in these experiments has been perpetual, while that of real anæsthetics has been so partial and temporary as scarcely to afford a reduction of twenty per cent. on the agony normally produced by the manglings undergone by the victims;

3rd, That no less than twenty-four American physiologists contributed to the vast sum of suffering we have registered, namely :—Dr. Austin Flint (New York) ; Dr. Isaac Ott (Pennsylvania) ; G. B. Woodfield ; Dr. H. Newell Martin (Johns Hopkins University) ; Edward Mussey Hartwell ; Dr. G. M. Garland (Harvard) ; Dr. Christian Sihler (Johns Hopkins University) ; Dr. W. Councilman (Johns Hopkins University) ; Dr. H. O. Bowditch (Harvard) ; Dr. Henry Sewell (Michigan) ; Dr. D. W. Steiner (Michigan) ; Dr. J. W. Warren (Harvard) ; Dr. H. A. Hare ; Dr. Wood ; Dr. Reichert ; Dr. Randall Hutchinson (Pennsylvania) ; William S. Carter ; Dr. B. A. Watson

(Jersey City) ; H. H. Donaldson (Johns Hopkins University) ; Lewis J. Stevens ; Dr. N. Senn (Chicago) ; Dr. Harold C. Ernst (Harvard) ; Dr. Beyer ; and Dr. W. S. Halsted (New York).

4th. At least five great States of the Union, viz., New York, Massachusetts, Michigan, Illinois, and Pennsylvania, contain among their noble educational, religious and charitable institutions, a score of chambers wherein the Art of Torture has been carried to a perfection which the "devildoms of Spain" in the old days of the Inquisition could not equal in ingenuity or pitilessness.

Men and Women of America! Suffer us who are laboring to stop vivisection in our own country, to plead with you for its suppression in your younger land, where as yet the new vice of scientific cruelty cannot be deeply rooted. An appeal has just been made to you in one of your foremost periodicals* to subscribe out of your private resources to support physiological laboratories for the sake of the utility of vivisection to surgery. How fallacious is that plea we leave to be set forth by such experts as our own illustrious surgeon, Mr. Lawson Tait,† whose great contributions to the progress of surgery the author himself acknowledges. But whether the practice be useful or useless, we ask you to reflect whether it be *morally lawful* —(not to speak of humane, or generous, or manly)—to seek to relieve our own pains at the cost of such unutterable anguish as has been already inflicted on unoffending creatures in the name of Science? You now know, to a

* Art. *Recent Progress in Surgery*, by Dr. W. W. Keen. *Harper's Magazine*, October, 1889.

† See *Uselessness of Vivisection*, by Lawson Tait, F.R.C.S., &c., pp. 41, Offices of Victoria Street Society, 20, Victoria Street, London.

certain extent, *what it is* that the advocates of vivisection really mean when they ask you to endow "Research." Will you—bearing their experiments in mind—*pay* them to repeat such cruelties?

We look forward with hope and confidence to find that the hour wherein the intelligence of America awakens to the true nature of Vivisection, will be the hour of the condemnation thereof by your consciences, and the prohibition thereof by your laws.

THE END.